jE

Duncan Rumplemeyer's BAD Birthday

For three Duncans:
Craig Hooker, Chris Keslar, and Kirsten Silverstein

SIMON & SCHUSTER BOOKS FOR YOUNG READERS
An imprint of Simon & Schuster Children's Publishing Division
1230 Avenue of the Americas, New York, New York 10020
SIMON & SCHUSTER BOOKS FOR YOUNG READERS is a trademark of
Simon & Schuster, Inc.
Book design by Lee Wade
The text for this book is set in Filosofia.
The illustrations for this book are rendered
in gouache and ink on bristol board.
Manufactured in China
2 4 6 8 10 9 7 5 3 1
Library of Congress Cataloging-in-Publication Data
Stadler, Alexander.
Duncan Rumplemeyer's bad birthday / Alexander Stadler.—1st ed.
p. cm.
"A Paula Wiseman Book."
Summary: Duncan does not understand such things as why dessert must
be eaten last or why people should share, and on his mischievous days,
like one particular birthday, he has a hard time paying attention to rules.
ISBN 0-689-86732-8
[1. Birthdays—Fiction. 2. Behavior—Fiction. 3. Rules (Philosophy)—
Fiction.] I. Title.
PZ7.S7754 Du 2004
[Fic]—dc22
2003014845

Duncan Rumplemeyer's BAD Birthday

ALEXANDER STADLER

A PAULA WISEMAN BOOK
Simon & Schuster Books for Young Readers
New York London Toronto Sydney

My name is DUNCAN RUMPLEMEYER, and I am not a bad kid—but sometimes I act like one.

Some days I wake up feeling mischievous, and on those days it's hard for me to pay attention to the rules. On mischievous days I keep asking myself, "Why?"

Why take naps? Why go to sleep when you can play Crash Test?

Chocolate cake is delicious and chicken tastes boring, so why do you have to eat all of your chicken and not all of the cake? Why do I have to stop at one slice? What good is one tiny slice? Who cares about one tiny slice?

Also, there is sharing. Sharing makes no sense at all. Why share? If a toy is fun, why let go of it? Who knows when you'll get it back?

One time I shared my stranglehold-lock master action figure with Flora Ingraham, and she took it and stuck it in the toilet.

And when my father forced me to share my foaming toothpaste with Brian Fenwick, Brian swallowed half the tube and then was sick in four out of the five rooms in our house. Sharing isn't even good for the people you share with.

I just don't get it. But usually, even though I don't
understand why I'm supposed to follow the rules, I
follow them anyway. The problem is that today was one
of my mischievous days and it was also my birthday.

The trouble started last night.

I was lying in bed, dreaming a nice dream, when all of a sudden I woke up and thought, *Presents are in this house.* I checked the clock. It was *almost* my birthday. . . .

My mother
was not
pleased.

Instead of my special birthday breakfast of egg-muffin delicious, my mother just gave me cereal. Usually after breakfast we sit around and open the presents and talk about them and play with them.

But I was being punished, so there weren't any presents to talk about.

It didn't matter, though, because my party started a little while later, and everybody brought more presents. Howard Banister gave me a machine that makes all kinds of rude sounds, and Flora got me that monster-making machine with the gel. Then there was a clown.

All of the grown-ups laughed at him. Why do they do that? Why do they laugh when something isn't funny? My father had hired the clown, and he asked me if I liked him. I didn't want to say something that wasn't true, so I told him, "No."

Then he got mad at me too.

After the clown left, we all went to the park to play.

I piled up my new presents and dragged them to the park. Flora kept wanting to TOUCH everything. I told her to back off. My mother gave me a look.

When we got there, I started to put together my sound machine. My father wasn't in the mood to help me, so I had to do it by myself.

It took a really long time. When I finally finished, I looked up—and what did I see?

Everyone was playing with

MY PRESENTS!

Flora, Howard . . . even the Mancuso twins!
Everyone was messing around with my stuff! My
parents tried to stop me, but it was no use. I grabbed
back every single toy.

After that everybody went home.

Then I was thrown into PRISON.

My parents said that people who don't share have no friends. They said that if I really wanted to have my presents to myself so badly, then I could spend the rest of the afternoon with them, trapped in my room. Alone.

It really didn't seem like a punishment. I played with my new toys and made a gel creature.

I even invented a new rude noise that sounded kind of squishy. But there was no one there to hear it. If you make a rude noise and no one hears it, is it still gross?

After forty-five minutes of playing, it got to be less fun. After an hour and a half I started to feel lonely. I thought about trying to escape. But where could I go? All of my friends were mad at me. Flora was disgusted.

When my father brought me my snack, I asked if I was allowed one phone call.

I called Flora. I told her I was sorry for snatching away all of the toys the way I did.

Flora told me I was a selfish baby, and then she accepted my apology.

After I hung up, my mother told me that I could invite Flora over for dinner if I wanted to.

We had egg-muffin delicious. After dinner Flora and I played with the noisemaker.

I learned a lot of things today, but the most important thing I learned is this. . . . A disgusting sound is a lot more disgusting if somebody's there to hear it.